A LITTLE BIT CRAZY

KNIGHT SECURITY
BOOK 1

SHAW HART

WANT A FREE BOOK?

You can grab Sweets **Here.**
**Check out my website, www.shawhart.com for
more free books!**

*

I might be a little bit crazy.

I mean, I think jumping out of planes is fun, so there must be something a little off with me, but I've got nothing on Quinn Walder.

She rear-ends me and then asks me to be her boyfriend.

Her *fake* boyfriend.

Who does that?

She's got to be nuts, but if she is, then so am I because I just agreed to her crazy plan.

Now, what happens when this fake relationship starts to feel real?

ONE

Rhett

ANSON IS busy typing away on his phone, his brown hair hanging in his eyes.

He needs a haircut. When we were in the SEALs, he would never have his hair that long.

I run my fingers through my black hair and realize that I might need a trim too. I sigh, turning back to my best friend, but he's still distracted. We're supposed to be finishing up paperwork for a client, but I guess I'll be taking care of that.

I turn to interrupt him, but when he grins, I turn away again. I'm sure he's texting my sister, Lottie, and I don't even want to guess what they might be discussing.

I'm actually glad that Anson and Lottie finally got together. I had been watching them dance around their feelings for each other since we were teenagers. I hated thinking that I was the reason why they weren't together and happy.

It took me being hospitalized for Anson to finally have

the conversation with me, but that was months ago, and things seem to be running smoothly ever since.

"Have you heard from Whit and Hunter lately?" Anson asks as I log out of my computer.

"Yeah, they got Anise back safely. They're all still getting settled in Fallen Peak."

"Think we'll get invited to the wedding?" He asks as he grabs his jacket and stands.

"Maybe. Do you want to go? Lottie will be pretty pregnant by then," I remind him.

"Yeah, she probably won't be able to travel that far. We'll send a gift."

I nod, joining him as he heads for the door. We talked in the hospital about what to do after I was injured overseas. Anson and I were both Navy SEALs, but neither of us wanted to go back after I was hurt and we found out that Lottie was pregnant. So, instead, we opened our own security company.

There are always a ton of people and companies looking for security in Los Angeles, and business has been booming since we opened Knight Security a few months ago. We've actually been talking about hiring more people already, and I have a few candidates in mind.

I stretch out my shoulders as I walk and sigh when I see Anson giving me a worried look. My left shoulder and side have been a little stiff since the attack that brought me back stateside. Anson and Lottie have been hovering over me, treating me like I'm on my deathbed. Things improved when we all got our own separate places, but that hasn't stopped Lottie from stopping by to check on me and Anson from asking how I'm doing every time I see him.

"I'm fine," I say before he can say anything, and he grins.

"Sure, you are. You know, I was thinking," he starts, and I groan.

"That can be dangerous," I quip, and he rolls his eyes.

"I have great ideas."

"Name one."

"Oh, shut up. I was thinking that maybe I could set you up with someone, and we could try a double date," he finishes, and I bite back another groan.

This is my second problem. Now that Lottie and Anson are all blissed out and in love, they want me to be too. They've been dropping hints about cool date places or pointing out pretty girls.

I suppose this shouldn't really be categorized as a problem. My friend and sister are happy and in love and they just want that for me too. It should be a good thing.

Except that dating isn't really my focus right now. I want our new company to be a success. I want to make sure I'm fully healed and okay mentally and physically before I try to settle down.

How do I explain that to them without making them worry even more than they already are about me?

"Who are you going to set me up with?" I ask as we stop next to his truck.

"I'm sure that I know some single women."

"Yeah, we know all of the same women, and the only one who is single is Goldie."

"Okay, so, Goldie."

"Goldie is Lottie's best friend, and she's like a little sister to me. Besides, you know she's secretly in love with her Boss Man."

"So, you pretend to date her, and it nudges him into taking action," he says with a shrug.

"So, in this scenario, I'm not finding love so much as being used?"

"Maybe it will lead to love."

"Yeah, a *brotherly* love," I stress.

"So damn picky."

"Oh my god, why are we friends?" I ask, staring up at the sky.

"Cause no one else wanted to be," he says, punching my shoulder.

That's kind of the truth. Lottie, Anson, and I grew up on the wrong side of the tracks. Our parents were neglectful or downright abusive in some way, and we spent more time looking after each other than they did. We made sure that Lottie was safe and secure in our apartment before we joined the military, and we haven't looked back since. We formed our own family, and it's been the best decision I've ever made.

"I should be getting home."

"Tell Lottie that I said hi," I say, and he nods.

"Will do. See you tomorrow!"

He waves, and I wave back as I turn to head to my car. Knight Security is in a building downtown, and I'm not looking forward to battling traffic on my way back to my apartment. It doesn't matter where you are in Los Angeles, though. There's just no way to avoid it.

I moved out of the apartment I shared with Lottie and Anson just last month, and I'm still getting settled in my new place. I debate stopping for food, but I'm tired. I want to get home and take a shower. Then I'll focus on what to eat.

I turn out of the parking lot and inch my way toward First Street. As soon as I turn onto the road, I jerk forward.

"Son of a..." I trail off as I realize that I've been rear-ended.

Great. This is just what I needed today.

I rub my shoulder, trying to ease the ache starting back up there as I unbuckle and slip out of the car.

"I'm so sorry! The sun got in my eyes, and well, that's no excuse. Here let me get my insurance," comes the sweetest voice I've ever heard.

It's not a Los Angeles accent, and I try to place it. My eyes snap to the woman bent half in and half out of the driver's side door, and I can't hold in the moan when I see her round ass waving in my face.

"Goddamn," I mutter to myself.

I take a step closer to her, my eyes devouring her curves hungrily when she finally fishes out the insurance card and turns to face me.

"Here we are," she says, and my eyes roam over her.

"Are you alright?" I ask, and her pale green eyes snap to mine.

"I'm... fine. I'm fine," she says, clearing her throat.

Her eyes go to the back of my car, and she winces when she sees the bumper hanging down to the ground.

"A lot better than your car. I really am so sorry," she says, and I take another step toward her.

"What's your name?"

"Oh, right. Here's the card. I'm Quinn Walder."

"It's nice to meet you, Quinn," I say, reaching out and taking the card from her.

Our fingers touch, and a tingle races up my arm and down my spine. My gaze locks with hers, and I wonder if she felt it too.

"I'm Rhett," I say when the silence has stretched between us for too long.

"Let me call my insurance company," she says and she turns away from me.

I want to call her back, to feel her name on my lips, to have her eyes and attention back on me, but she's already grabbed her phone.

I guess maybe she can't feel this connection between us after all.

TWO

Quinn

THIS IS JUST MY LUCK.

My day was already a flaming disaster, but sure, let's add a car accident to the mix.

I had just left my parents' house, where they once again tried to force one of their friends' kids on me. It's still been an adjustment getting used to my parents actually taking an interest in me. They had sent me off to boarding school when I was a tween, and before that, a long string of nannies took care of me.

Now that I'm older, they seem to have remembered that they have a child. Unfortunately for me, they only seem to care about who they can marry me off to. It apparently has to be one of their boring friends' spawn. I'm sure they think the world would fall apart if I happened to marry outside of our social class.

Unfortunately for them, I'm not interested in anyone that they set me up with. I want to marry for love. Besides,

I'm not interested in settling down right now or dating. I just got out of college, and I'm excited to be starting this next chapter in my life. I want to focus on building my career.

I might just change my mind though if my parents' had tried to set me up with someone like Rhett.

I shouldn't be ogling the poor guy. I mean, I just rear-ended him. He looks tired, and I'm sure he was anxious to get home before I derailed that.

Still, what would it be like to be with a guy like that? One who looks like he stepped off the cover of a magazine.

Black hair matches the rest of his outfit, but it's his eyes that draw me in. They're a dark blue, and they just seem so insightful, like he can see right through me.

I wonder where he's from. I wonder what he does for a living. I'd love to photograph him. I'd do color pictures only so that I can capture his tan skin and those beautiful eyes.

He's wearing a pair of black camo pants and a plain black t-shirt. He looks like he's in the military, and I bite my bottom lip as my eyes caress all his muscles.

"Marines?" I blurt out, and he blinks.

"No, Navy."

"SEAL?"

"Yep, what gave it away?"

"The fifteen-pack," I tell him, and he laughs, looking down at his abs.

I can just make out the ridges through his shirt, and my mouth waters at the sight.

"Policy number," comes a voice in my ear, and I startle.

"Uh, just a second."

I fumble with the insurance card and hurry to read off my policy number. I had completely forgotten that I was on the phone with them. I was too distracted by Rhett.

He's smiling knowingly at me now, and I realize I showed him my cards when I mentioned his abs. Now it's obvious that I was checking him out.

I can't help but compare him to the man my parents had picked for me today. Tripp. What a pretentious name. It suited him to a T.

The guy was a classic frat boy type, popped-up collar and all. We have nothing in common. Well, nothing except rich parents.

I wish my parents had considered what I wanted when they tried to set me up. That would require that they knew me at all, though.

I need to figure out some way to put a stop to all of this matchmaking; I think, as the insurance company places me on a brief hold. *Maybe if I find my own boyfriend, they would get the message. Could I hire someone to do that? Like an escort but without the sex.*

That way, my parents would get the message that I don't need or want their help picking a partner. Maybe it would scare off Tripp too.

Maybe I should just travel. That's my dream, to be a travel blogger. I've lived a pretty sheltered life, though, and I'm concerned that I don't have the street smarts to travel alone.

I bet a Navy SEAL could keep me safe...

Maybe it's time that I took the chance though.

The insurance lady comes back on the line, and I give her my information and tell her about the accident before I pass the phone to Rhett. I listen to his deep voice as he reads off his own insurance company and policy.

"The tow truck should be here soon," he tells me, and I wince.

"Can I give you a ride somewhere?" I offer.

"I have to go with them to the shop, but thanks."

"I'm really so sorry."

"It's okay. I'm just glad that no one was hurt."

"Me too. Here let me give you my number in case you need anything with the car."

He passes me his phone, and I type in my number, hitting the call button so I have his too.

The tow truck pulls up, and I wait around until they have his car loaded up. My car has a dent in the front bumper, and I'll have to get that fixed at some point, but it's still drivable.

"Sorry again," I say as Rhett gets ready to hop in the tow truck, and he smiles.

"No worries. See you around, Quinn."

"See you, Rhett," I say quietly as I slip behind the wheel of my Mercedes.

I drive through downtown traffic, letting out a sigh of relief when I pull into my parking spot outside of my apartment. My parents gifted it to me when I graduated from college. I thought it was sweet, but now I realize it's their way of still keeping me under their thumb.

That fake boyfriend idea is starting to sound better and better.

I freeze halfway into my apartment as a wonderful idea occurs to me.

Would he agree to it, though?

Rhett

BY THE TIME I get my car arranged at the repair shop and make it back home in my rental car, it's close to nine at night. I'm exhausted and starving as I head into my apartment and head straight for the shower. The plan is to rinse off, scarf down some food, and then pass out.

That plan is once again derailed by Quinn Walder.

This time she's calling instead of hitting my car with hers. I can't believe she's calling me, and my first thought is that maybe she felt something for me too. That thought is quickly squashed by reality.

She probably just needs something for the car insurance.

"Hello?" I answer before it can go to voicemail.

"Rhett!" She says, slurring slightly, and I become concerned.

I don't know this girl at all, but I got the impression that she wasn't much of a drinker. She seemed too innocent for that.

"Are you single?" She asks, and I can't help but laugh.

"This is a weird way to get out of paying for the damage to my car," I joke, and she laughs, the sound light and infectious in my ear.

"Nooo," she insists. "I promise I'll pay for that, but I was hoping to ask you for a favor."

Even drunk, she sounds so sophisticated. I can tell she has money and probably comes from a rich family, and I wonder what we could have in common.

"Have you been drinking?" I ask, trying to figure out just how drunk she is.

"A little, but I swear it's a good idea!"

"Okay, I'll bite. What's the favor?" I ask.

Please let it be that you want me to come over and make you come so many times that you go hoarse from screaming my name and pass out.

"Well," she starts, and I listen as she takes a deep breath to compose herself. "Would you be my fake boyfriend? Just for a little bit!"

Fake boyfriend?

This isn't exactly what I was hoping for. I wonder why she wants a fake boyfriend when I'm sure she could get a real one in a second.

I haven't been able to stop thinking about Quinn since I left in the tow truck. There was just something about the curvy girl that called to me. I'm not joking when I say there was a connection between us.

I wish she felt it too and wanted to go out with me for real, but this could be my way in with her. My original plan was to give it a day or two and then call and ask her out to dinner, but this could work too.

Maybe it is a good idea, though. It would probably help me get Anson and Lottie off my case.

Still, I should probably know what I'm getting myself into.

"Why do you want a fake boyfriend?" I ask her, even though I want to agree on the spot.

"I... I need my parents to get off of my case, and I'm hoping they'll stop setting me up with guys named Tripp."

"Who's Tripp?" I ask, getting instantly jealous of a guy I've never even met.

"The latest guy in a long line of pretentious dicks that my parents have been trying to set me up with," she says with a long, drawn-out sigh.

"And you don't want any of them?"

I know the answer, but I need to hear her say that.

"God, no! They're all so dreadful."

She's still slurring her words, so I lay down a new challenge instead of saying yes.

"Alright, if you remember this conversation in the morning, I'll be your fake boyfriend."

"Deal," she says, sounding sleepy.

"Goodnight, Quinn," I say, grinning as I end the call.

Man, I hope she remembers this.

I hop in the shower, quickly rinsing off before I practically inhale a sandwich and crash into my bed. When I fall asleep, for the first time in a long time, it's with a smile on my face.

Quinn

I GROAN as I roll over in bed the next morning. I'm not really a drinker, but when I got home last night, it just seemed like a good idea.

What started as me just needing some liquid courage to work up the nerve to call him and tell him about my plan kind of got away from me. By the time I actually did call, I was a little more than tipsy.

Still, when I wake up the next morning, the first thing I think about is him and our phone call last night.

He didn't outright tell me no or laugh in my face. That has to be a good sign, right?

I chew on my bottom lip as I debate if I should call him again now or wait until later. I still think it's a good idea, but I'm not feeling as confident this morning as I was last night.

Maybe that will change once I get rid of this pounding headache.

I find the courage to crawl out of bed and head into the

bathroom. I spend my time in the shower trying not to throw up. When I stumble out of the shower and get a look at my reflection, I feel like heading back to bed.

I'm so pale that I look like death. Dark circles are under my eyes, and I sigh as I splash some cold water on my face.

Maybe going back to bed isn't a bad idea. It's not like I have anything else going on today.

I need to get more pictures for my blog. I've been trying to find unique and trendy spots to feature in the area since I don't feel comfortable traveling solo just yet.

I had planned to go down to Chinatown to look around with my camera, but being anywhere near the sun right now seems like a terrible idea.

I crash back down onto the mattress, wrapping the blanket around my naked body as I burrow under the pillows.

"That's better."

My eyes close, and I'm planning on sleeping off this hangover when my phone rings.

Maybe it's Rhett.

"Ugh," I growl when I see my mom's name on the screen instead.

I can't deal with her right now so I let it go to voicemail and try to go back to sleep. When she calls again, I give up and hit ignore, dialing Rhett's number instead.

"Morning," he says, and he sounds so fresh and hot.

"Hi," I croak out.

I clear my throat, but I don't think that it will help much. I need about a gallon of coffee and a few more hours of sleep to sound human again.

"How are you feeling?" He asks.

"I'm never drinking again."

"That's what they all say," he says with a laugh.

"I remember," I blurt out, and his laugh cuts off.

"Can you meet me for coffee? This feels like a conversation that we should have in person."

"Go outside?" I whine, and he cracks up.

"I know it's hard, but there will be coffee there. Nice, hot coffee," he tempts me, and I sigh.

"Fine. I'll get dressed and brave the outside."

"I'm honored," he tells me.

"Where am I going?"

"There's a little café over on Fifth Street."

"I know it," I say

"Meet there in half an hour?"

"Alright," I say, trying not to groan.

"See you soon."

He ends the call, and I close my eyes as I crawl out of bed and head over to the closet. I should probably get dressed up, make myself look as hot as possible so that he actually agrees to this crazy plan, but I just don't have the energy for that right now.

I grab a loose-fitting tunic and a pair of my comfiest yoga pants before I pad down the hall to the kitchen, where I promptly down an entire glass of water.

"Not better," I groan when my stomach revolts.

Alright, let's get this over with.

I head out the door, slipping on my sunglasses in the elevator and hissing when I step outside, and the sun tries to blind me.

With the L.A. traffic, it takes me closer to forty minutes to get there, and I head inside to see Rhett already waiting for me. He's sitting at a table away from the windows, and I'm instantly grateful that he picked a spot away from the sun.

"You made it," he says with a charming smile as he stands to greet me.

"Barely," I croak, and he shoots me a sympathetic look.

"Do you want something to eat or drink?" He offers, and I cover my mouth with my hand.

"Not quite yet," I say when the threat of puking all over the hottest man I've ever met passes.

"Gotcha."

He takes a sip of his drink, eyeing me over the rim, and I focus on meeting his eyes without blushing.

"So, are we fake dating?" I ask when the silence stretches on too long.

"About that..."

I still can't believe that he's actually agreeing to this or even thinking about it. I know why I need a fake boyfriend, but this guy could walk into any bar or club, close his eyes, point at someone, and get a girlfriend. Why does he need a fake relationship?

"You don't have to agree, of course. It would help me out, but I'm sure you have better things to do," I say, already moving to stand.

"Wait! I kind of need a fake girlfriend, too," he admits quietly, and I blink, plopping back down into my seat.

"Why? You're..." I trail off, waving my hand at his impressive physique.

"I just got out of the military. I was medically discharged after an ambush. My best friend and sister are worried about me. They're also together now and seem to want me to be just as happy and head over heels in love as they are."

"And you don't want that?"

"I'm not sure that I have time for it right now. Anson and I just started our own security company a few months ago, and we're still getting it all setup. Adding anything else to my plate right now just doesn't seem feasible."

"We make time for the things that are important to us," I whisper more to myself, but Rhett hears and gives me a sad look.

"We do. Dating just isn't important to me right now."

We share a look, and I feel like maybe this could actually work. It would benefit both of us, and it doesn't have to be forever.

"If we do this, we should have some ground rules," I say, and Rhett sits up straighter.

"What kind of rules?"

"Like a timeline. We'll have an end date where we 'break up.' We have to have so many 'dates' a week or something."

"Okay, I can agree with that. What else?" He asks, and I bite my lip, trying to think of other ground rules.

"Um, no dating anyone else or sleeping with anyone else during that time."

"I wouldn't," he says, and I nod.

"Me either."

"Okay, so we agree on those rules. What else?"

"I don't know. I guess we can add more as we go?"

He nods, and I look around the busy café.

"We should get our background story straight and maybe some key facts about each other so if anyone asks, we're all on the same page."

"Well, I'm Rhett St. James. I was a Navy SEAL up until about five months ago. I was deployed and my unit was ambushed. I was shot and sent back to the VA hospital here. I got out after that."

He pushes some of his hair out of his eyes, and I notice

then that his left shoulder seems a little stiff. I'm guessing that's where he was injured.

"I'm Quinn Walder. My parents are well off, and they keep trying to set me up with their well-off friends' sons."

"And you don't want that?"

"No, not at all. They're all so stuck up and boring. I don't want that life."

"Are your parents going to be okay with us dating? I don't come from money. Not even close. My parents were addicts and abusive assholes."

"Rhett," I start.

"It's okay. I don't see or talk to them anymore. My sister and I survived that and we're okay," he rushes to add, but I still feel uneasy.

My heart is breaking for a young Rhett who had to deal with all of that. My parents weren't present or super active in my life, but they always were able to provide for me, and I never had to worry about them hitting me or anything.

"I'm sorry you had to deal with that," I say honestly.

"I know. It's okay," he says again, and I nod.

"I don't know how they'll react when I introduce you to them, but I'm hoping they'll back off if they see that you're sticking around. I just need to buy myself some time to get my blog off of the ground and then hopefully, I'll be traveling a lot and won't have to see them that often."

"What blog?" Rhett asks with interest, and it catches me off guard.

It's the first time I've told someone my plans where the person has shown interest or been supportive of it in any way. It's nice, but maybe a little sad that it's a stranger that is the first person to do that for me.

"I started a travel blog. I went to art school for photography, and my dream is to travel the world and find cool spots to photograph. Maybe do some photo shoots every now and then," I say, and Rhett smiles.

"I bet you'd be good at that," he says with a bright smile, and my heart flips over in my chest.

I can tell that he really means that. He hasn't even seen any of my photos, but he means it. I've never had anyone believe in me so much.

"I've started it, but just with local spots. I know I need to branch out, I just... haven't gotten that far yet."

I can't seem to bring myself to admit to this fearless Navy SEAL that I'm afraid to travel anywhere alone. I know, deep down, that he wouldn't judge me. Rhett seems like the most supportive, kind man I've ever met, and I'm sure he'd understand, but I still can't say the words.

"Do your parents know about the blog?"

"No, not yet. They wouldn't be supportive," I admit, and he frowns but nods.

"Anything else I need to know?" He asks.

"I went to boarding school when I was younger. My favorite color is blue. I love seafood and moose track ice cream."

"I love seafood too," Rhett says, and I settle deeper into the chair across from him.

We talk about our favorite things for the next half an hour until his phone rings, and I realize I've probably taken up too much of his time already.

"I should let you go," I say, gathering up my things. "Oh, wait! We never talked about what we're going to say if anyone asks how we met."

"Why don't we keep it simple and as close to the truth as possible?" He suggests.

"So, I rear-ended you?"

"Yeah."

"Will that be enough time to show that this is a real relationship?" I ask, and Rhett shrugs.

"My friend and sister won't believe it's been for longer. We're pretty close, and they would think it was weird if we had been dating for longer."

"Okay, we might have to keep the ruse going for longer than."

"That works for me. We can tell everyone that you rear-ended me, and it was love at first sight for me," he says with a small smile, and for the first time all day, he seems a little nervous.

"Okay," I say, trying not to blush. "That works."

"I need to head back to the office," he says, almost apologetically, as he stands too.

"I, uh, there's an event at my parents' house this weekend. Would you be able to join me?" I ask. "I know that it's short notice."

"I'm free. I'll be there. My friend, Anson, has been asking about a double date. Are you free this week if he wants to set something up? I can see if he's free this Friday?"

"That works."

"Cool."

He smiles at me, and for some reason, my brain decides that now is the right time to show him how much of a dork I am. I thrust my hand out into the space between us, and he seems caught off guard, but he reaches out, his big, strong hand wrapping around mine and shaking for the both of us.

His hand is so warm against mine. The calluses on his fingertips rub against the back of my hand, sending shivers down my spine.

"I'll see you Friday then," Rhett says, and I nod.

"See you then."

We head out, and I can't help but take one last glance back at him as I climb into my car. He's looking back at me, his dark blue eyes sparkling in the sun as he grins at me and climbs into his car.

Butterflies take flight in my stomach, and I smile to myself as I start my car and head home.

FIVE

Rhett

"I'M EXCITED to meet your new girl," Lottie says as she gets out of Anson's truck.

"Yeah, I'm glad that we were able to set this up so fast," Anson says.

I just nod. I've been texting with Quinn for the last few days, getting this double date set up, and trying to learn everything I can about my new girlfriend. *Fake* girlfriend.

I feel like I need to keep making that distinction, just to myself, so that I don't forget that this isn't real. Things with Quinn are so easy and natural that it's easy to forget that we're not really together. This isn't a real date.

We're at the boardwalk, and I glance around, wondering if Quinn is already here, but I don't see her anywhere. I had wanted to drive her, but she texted me an hour ago to say that she had lost track of time and would just meet us here.

Anson is distracted by Lottie, and I'm grateful. He's

been asking me a ton of questions these last few days about Quinn. I told him as close to the truth as possible. That she was the one to rear-end me, but I think she could be the one.

It's the truth, so it's not like I'm lying to my best friend or sister.

Instead, it feels like I'm lying to Quinn and myself by calling this a fake relationship.

Platinum blonde hair catches my eye, and I turn, smiling, when I see Quinn weaving her wave through the small crowd waiting to get tickets and head onto the boardwalk.

"Hey! Sorry, I'm late," she says, hesitating slightly before she rises up onto her tiptoes and wraps her arms around my neck in a hug.

"No worries," I say, my own arms going to her waist and pulling her against me.

We never really talked about acting like a couple the other day at the café, just basic facts about each other. I didn't even think about being able to hold her hand or hug her.

Will she let me kiss her?

I don't want to let her go, but she sinks back to her feet, and I'm forced to take a step back. I clear my throat before I turn back to Anson and Lottie.

"Guys, this is Quinn. Quinn, this is my sister, Lottie, and my best friend, Anson."

"It's so nice to meet you," Quinn says, shaking both of their hands.

"You too!" Lottie says, and I can tell by her smile that she likes Quinn already. "I love your outfit. That top is so cute."

"Oh, thanks," Quinn says and seems caught off guard by the compliment.

I wonder why? She's beautiful. She has to know that.

"Are we ready to go on some rides?" Anson asks with a huge grin, and he grabs Lottie's hand, pulling her along beside him.

"You look beautiful," I whisper down to Quinn, and she smiles.

"Thanks. I wasn't sure what to wear. I think I tried on ten different outfits," she admits, and I smile.

It's nice to know that I'm not the only one who was a little nervous and anxious for our date tonight.

I'm dressed similarly to Quinn in jeans and a sweater, but my sweatshirt is black, and hers is a pale pink. Her platinum blonde hair is pulled back into a high ponytail that swishes between her shoulder blades with each step.

Her cheeks are a little flushed from the cool evening breeze, and her pretty green eyes are bright and filled with happiness as she looks around.

"I've never been here before," she tells me, and I'm surprised.

"Didn't you grow up here in Los Angeles?"

"Yeah, but my parents didn't really take me on trips down to the pier... or the beach," she says, looking over the side of the pier at the waves crashing down on the shore.

"Where did you go instead?"

"Paris or London. Anywhere that was deemed the next *It* spot. Though they stopped taking me with them when I was about eight, so I don't really remember the trips."

"What happened after you turned eight?" I ask.

"I was sent to boarding school."

"Oh, right. Did you like boarding school?"

"It was fine. It was kind of a lot like being home," she admits.

"How so?"

"I was alone," she says quietly, and I tense, my hand reaching for hers to try to offer comfort.

"I'm sorry, Quinn."

"It's fine," she says, waving me off.

I still want to talk about it, but Lottie and Anson turn back to us then. I can see that Quinn is grateful for the interruption, so I decide to let it go. I should be keeping things light between us anyway.

"What should we go on first?" Lottie asks.

"What are you allowed to go on?" I ask her, and Quinn frowns.

"What?" Quinn asks, and Lottie smiles at her.

"I'm pregnant, and these two are determined to keep me from having fun. I can go on the Ferris wheel and play the games," she insists, pulling her black hair over one shoulder.

"Okay, Ferris wheel it is then," Anson says, leading us that way.

We join the end of the line, and I turn to face Quinn.

"What did you do today?" I ask her.

"I went and looked around town. I feel like a tourist after not being here for a few years. It's crazy how much has changed."

"I bet," I say. "Quinn is an amazing photographer. She's starting a travel blog," I tell Anson and Lottie.

"Really? That's so cool! You'll have to send me the link. I want to check it out."

"Sure," Quinn says, and I see her trying not to squirm under my praise or Lottie's interest.

It's obvious that Quinn isn't used to people paying so much attention to her. I'm guessing she flew under the radar at home and school. I'd like to spoil her by giving her all of my attention, and I wonder if it would freak her out if I told her that.

We move up in line, and Quinn turns to Anson and Lottie.

"How did you two meet?" She asks them as I move closer to her and wrap my arm around her shoulder.

It must be warm against my side, or maybe she's just trying to sell this fake relationship because she cuddles closer to me. I breathe in her sweet honeysuckle scent and it makes me want to lick her.

"We were actually friends when we were younger. Anson and Rhett were best friends for as far back as I can remember, and we were close too," Lottie says.

"Aww, that must have been nice. When did you start dating?"

"Only a few months ago. It took this one a while to admit that he wanted me," she says, laughing as she elbows Anson in the side.

"Something like that," he says, smiling down at her softly.

"It was exactly like that," I groan, and Quinn laughs. "It took them *years* to stop dancing around each other and finally admit they loved each other. It was so frustrating to watch."

"We didn't want to mess up our relationship with you," Anson argues, and he shakes his head.

It's our turn now, and Lottie and Anson step up first, climbing into their cart. Then it's our turn.

"I should have asked, but are you afraid of heights or anything?" I ask Quinn, and she smiles.

"No, at least, I don't think so."

"Guess we're going to find out," I joke, and she laughs.

"If I start clawing at you like a cat in a bath, that will be your sign that I don't like heights," she teases, and I laugh as we start to rise up into the sky.

"Are you having fun so far?" I ask her as the wheel starts to turn.

"Yeah, I really like Lottie and Anson. They seem so perfect together, and they're both so nice. I haven't had a fun night out like this in... well, forever," she says with a little laugh.

I point out some of the other rides, and I'm not surprised that she's never been on any of them. I promise her we'll try all of them, even if Lottie and Anson can't join us as we climb off the Ferris wheel and make our way over to the concession stand.

"Are you hungry?"

"Starving," she says as her eyes devour the menu.

"Want me to just get a little of everything and we can share?" I offer, and she smiles sweetly at me.

"That would be perfect."

"We're going to go grab that table," Lottie says, grabbing Quinn's hand and pulling her over to a just freed up picnic table.

"She's cool," Anson says when we're alone, and I smile.

"I know."

He laughs, and I step up to place my order. He orders after me, and I grab the drinks, heading over to the girls before I head back for the food. It's a ton of junk food, but I want Quinn to have this experience. We'll probably all get sick from eating so much fried food, but it will be worth it to be the first one to show this to Quinn.

"Dig in," I say as I set the food down in front of us.

"Thanks," Quinn says, and then she shocks the hell out of me by leaning over and brushing her lips against mine.

It's a quick kiss, there and gone in the blink of an eye,

but my lips keep buzzing as I grab my Coke and take a long drink.

I know it then. I'm already head over heels for this girl.

For my *fake* girlfriend.

Now I need to figure out how I can possibly make this fake relationship real.

SIX

Quinn

I'M in so much trouble.

This whole thing was meant to be fake. I mean, it was my own damn idea for it to be fake, but I already have real feelings for Rhett.

I can't believe I ever thought I would be able to keep things fake between us. Rhett is just so perfect that how could you not fall in love with him? He's handsome and sweet, supportive and funny. He makes me feel beautiful, smart and desired.

I don't need this right now. He's not part of any of my plans. Besides, I'm already so stressed out and on edge about my blog and parents that I don't think I can juggle one more thing.

Maybe I should call this whole thing off.

Except I don't think that would do any good. I already have feelings for Rhett. Pushing him away now is just going to hurt me.

I pace back and forth, chewing on my fingernail as I wait for Rhett to pick me up. We're supposed to be heading over to the house for whatever charity event they're holding this month. I'm already dreading it. These events are always so dreadful and more about people showing off than helping the actual charity that we're all there to support.

My puffy, tulle dress is already driving me crazy, and I try to tamp down the sides. It doesn't work.

My mom picked this out for me, and I'm only wearing it to try to soften the blow when I show up with Rhett in tow tonight.

A knock comes at the door, and I take a deep breath as I go to answer it.

There's no going back now.

I swing the door open, and my jaw drops.

"Holy shit," I say, practically drooling as I take in the beauty that is Rhett in a perfectly fitted black suit.

"I can clean up well if I need to," he says with a chuckle, and I nod.

"I'll say."

"You look beautiful."

"Thanks," I say, grabbing my clutch and pulling the door shut behind me.

"Are you ready for this?" He asks as we head for the elevator.

"I think so," I say with a sigh.

"That bad, huh?"

"I'm just not sure how they'll react. I mean, they'll have to be gracious because we're in public, but I doubt that will stop them from pushing their choices on me all night."

He nods, leading me outside and over to his car. I give him directions as we navigate our way through the traffic and up into the Hollywood Hills. There's a valet working at the gate of my parents' property, and I try to roll my shoulders back and ease some of the tension starting there.

"It's going to be okay," Rhett whispers in my ear, and I take a deep breath, relaxing as Rhett takes my hand and we head into the house.

The party is in full swing, and I look around for my parents.

"Do you want to seek out your parents or let them bump into us?" Rhett asks as I look around the front sitting room.

"Let's do a round. I'm sure that we'll run into them."

Sure enough, as expected, my mother is posted up in the living room, holding court. I'm sure my father is in his study doing the same, and I paste on a smile as I lead Rhett in her direction.

"That's her?" He asks once we're closer, and I nod.

"Hey, mom," I say brightly, and she turns in my direction, her eyes locking on mine and Rhett's clasped hands.

"Quinn, darling," she says, her smile turning fake and brittle around the edges as she takes in Rhett. "Who is your friend?"

"This is my boyfriend, Rhett," I say, my voice barely wavering.

Rhett squeezes my hand in encouragement, and I relax slightly.

"It's nice to meet you, ma'am," Rhett says when my mom doesn't say anything.

"What do you do for a living, Rhett?" She asks, and he smiles blandly.

"I was in the SEALs, but I got out a few months ago and started my own security company with a buddy of mine."

"Oh, how... nice," she finishes lamely, and I want to drag Rhett out of there then.

"Thanks," he says, squeezing my hand to keep me from saying anything.

"Have you seen Tripp yet?" She asks, turning to me.

It's obvious that she's done speaking with Rhett, and I'm embarrassed with how she's behaving right now. She can have all the money in the world, but it still can't buy her any class.

"No, not yet. We just got here."

"I think that he's with your father in the study," she says, and I nod.

She turns back to her friends then, and I know I've been dismissed. I nod toward the kitchen doorway to Rhett, and he nods, letting me lead him in that direction.

"So, that was my mom," I say once we're somewhere a little more private.

"She seems, uh..." he trails off, and I laugh.

"Yeah," I finish for him, and he smiles.

"Should we meet your dad now?"

"I think we're going to need food and something to drink first."

"Lead the way."

I smile to myself, taking his hand and leading him closer to the kitchen door. Servers are coming in and out, and I swipe two goblets of water while Rhett handles the food.

"I have no idea what any of this is, but it looks good," he says, and I laugh.

"Let's see how it tastes."

We spend a few minutes sampling the different canapes that the servers bring out, and for the first time, I actually have fun at one of these events.

"Quinn, there you are," my father says, and I can tell by the look on his face that he's already spoken to my mother. "Who is your friend?"

"Dad, this is my boyfriend, Rhett. Rhett, this is my father, Alastair Walder."

"It's nice to meet you, sir," Rhett says politely.

"Uh huh," my dad murmurs, and I roll my eyes. "Tripp was looking for you."

"Right. Let's go see if we can find him," I tell Rhett, dragging him away from my father.

"I'm so sorry about them," I whisper to Rhett, and he just smiles.

"It's alright. I've experienced worse."

People are dancing in the great room, and I try to steer Rhett away from it, but of course, that's when my mom spots me and waves me over. Tripp is standing beside her, and I know before I get there that I'm going to be forced to dance with him.

"There you are, darling," my mom says. "Tripp was looking for a dancing partner, and I was hoping to learn more about your friend."

I know that's bullshit. They just want me with Tripp and are willing to deal with Rhett to get that.

"Hi, Tripp," I say reluctantly. "This is Rhett, my boyfriend."

"Hey," Rhett says, and I see Tripp size him up.

Rhett easily has fifty pounds of pure muscle on his side. Where Tripp is soft, Rhett is hard. They're night and day. Tripp's hair is almost as pale as my blonde hair and his eyes are a muddy brown. I don't know how anyone who saw them together would choose Tripp over Rhett. It's not even a competition.

"Let's dance," Tripp says, grabbing my wrist and dragging me off.

"Uh," I glance back at Rhett and see him glaring at Tripp.

His eyes meet mine, and I wave him off.

"I'm fine," I mouth to him.

He doesn't look happy about it but nods and stays with my mom.

"I thought that your parents were trying to set us up," Tripp says, sounding put out.

"Were they? Well, I'm taken now. Sorry," I say, and I know that Tripp can hear the insincerity in my voice.

His hands tighten on me, and I wince, trying to put some space between us.

"I'll be cutting in now," Rhett says from behind me, and I blink, finding myself in his arms.

"Thanks," I whisper when I see Tripp storm off.

"Anytime," Rhett says as he starts to sway with me in his arms.

I rest my hands on his chest and smile to myself as I dance with my boyfriend.

Fake boyfriend, I remind myself and sigh quietly as I wonder what I'm going to do with all of these feelings when everything comes crashing down.

SEVEN

Rhett

"I'M REALLY sorry for how they've been treating you," Quinn says, and I shrug.

"It's alright. No offense, but your parents' opinion of me doesn't really matter to me. I know that I'm a good person and that there's more to life than money," I assure her.

"No, it's not. I don't even know why I came, let alone why I dragged you here. They don't really like me either," she admits, and I frown down at her.

"I'm sure that that's not true."

"It is, or, well, they don't know me well enough to decide if they like me or not. I just wanted them to stop pushing their choice of men on me. I don't have anything in common with them, though. Maybe it's better if I let this relationship go. I seem to be the only one really trying here."

I hold her closer in my arms, rubbing her back slowly.

"I'm sorry, Quinn. They're idiots if they can't see how awesome you are."

She nods against me, and I try to think of something to lighten the mood.

I hate that Quinn is upset with her parents and how this night is going, and I wish I could do something. I know that nothing short of me going back in time and being born to a different family, a well-off one that runs in the same social circles as them, is going to make them accept me.

She had tried to warn me on the drive over that her mom and dad can be a little pretentious, but I guess that I was hoping deep down that I could win them over. As soon as we walked in here, I knew that wasn't going to happen.

"Did you grow up here?" I ask Quinn as we sway back and forth to the classical music.

"Yeah, well, sometimes. I was mostly away at boarding school and then college," she says with a shrug.

I nod, looking around at the ornate room. The entire house I grew up in could fit into this one room. There's so much space and so many different rooms, but the décor remains the same throughout. Every room and crevice screams old money and power. There's this vibe though, that none of the furniture is really there to be used, just envied. Like it's not practical, just expensive.

Tripp steps back over to where Quinn's mother is glaring at me, and Quinn moves closer to me.

"Do you want to get out of here?" I whisper in her ear, and she nods right away.

"Yes, please."

I take her hand in mine, and she giggles as we run out of the house and down the hill to the valet. I pass him my ticket and wrap my arms around Quinn as he goes to get it.

"Are you hungry?" I ask, and she shakes her head.

"My stomach is kind of in knots still," she says quietly,

and I nod, moving to open her door as my car is parked out front.

"I'll take you home."

I help her into the car and then go around to the driver's side, tipping the valet before I slide behind the wheel.

The drive back to Quinn's place is silent, and I hate it. I wish that tonight wasn't ending so soon. I don't want to leave her, not while she's upset, but it's more than that. I like Quinn, really like her. I think she could be the one for me, and I'm afraid that she's going to call this whole thing off. Maybe our fake relationship isn't worth the fight or headache that she's sure to get from her parents.

"What can I do to cheer you up?" I ask as we idle at a red light.

She takes a deep breath, mulling over the question, and I tighten my grip on the steering wheel as I wait for the light to turn green.

"I just want to forget about them and how disappointed we are with each other for a little bit," she finally says, and I nod.

"I can do that."

She turns in her seat, arching an eyebrow at me.

"Really? How?"

I just grin at her as I hit the gas.

EIGHT

Quinn

"SO?" Rhett asks with a wide grin, and I laugh.

"Alright, this is a pretty good distraction," I admit as I sink deeper into the sand.

The waves are crashing right in front of us, and I snuggle deeper into his suit coat as I lick my ice cream cone.

We're currently sitting on the beach, eating ice cream even though it's like fifty degrees out. Rhett insisted that ice cream could cure everything, and I had gone along with his crazy plan because I didn't want the night to end on such a sour note. Actually, I didn't want the night to end at all.

"Beach or mountains?" I ask him, and he hums as he licks his own ice cream cone.

I had gotten cookies and cream, but Rhett's mint chocolate chip is looking better and better with every lick. My mouth waters as I watch his tongue swipe up more ice cream.

God, I wish that I was that cone.

"Beach, I think. The mountains in Afghanistan were pretty, but I don't have the best memories tied to them," he admits, and I nod.

"I think I'd choose the beach too."

"Is that where you're going to go first for your travel blog? Some beach somewhere?"

"Maybe. It would be cool to see the pink sand beaches in the Bahamas or the black sand beach in Iceland."

"You could get a little jar of sand from each place you go to," he suggests, and I smile.

"That would be cool."

"I have one from Afghanistan and Iraq," he says, and I smile.

"Really?"

"Yeah, it started as a joke with my unit, but I still have them."

He shrugs, and I study him. He hasn't really told me all that much about his time in the military, and I hate to pry, but it seems like he's opening up a bit tonight. I wonder if he's just doing that to distract me and make me feel better. It fits with who he is.

Rhett is the best person that I've ever met. He's caring and sweet, patient, funny, generous, and smart.

"How the hell are you still single?" I blurt out, and he laughs.

"Well, we were deploying like every nine months or so. Being gone for so long wasn't the best for starting a new relationship."

"Still," I say, and he smiles.

"Okay, the truth?"

"Please."

"My parents weren't the best role models for lasting love. I spent my entire childhood protecting Lottie and myself from them when they were on one of their tears. As soon as we got out, I joined the military with Anson, and things have kind of been a whirlwind since then. I just haven't given dating much thought until recently."

My heart skips when he says those last two words, and I look away from him so that he can't see the hope and longing shining in my eyes.

"What about you?" He asks when I don't say anything.

"Well, going to an all-girls boarding school limits the number of boys to date," I try to joke, and he smiles. "Then, I don't know. No one ever really interested me when I was in college."

I want to tell him that no one has ever interested me before now, but what if I'm reading this wrong? I don't want to make it awkward between us, and the truth is that I'm just not confident or bold enough to come right out and admit that I want him.

"Did you always want to join the military?" I ask him, trying to get us back into safer territory.

"No, not always. There weren't a ton of options for us, though. Anson and I both grew up with next to nothing. We've been scraping by our entire life, and the military was just the best option to change that."

Here I am, always bringing up my boarding school and fancy art college, and he had to risk his life just to make a living.

"So, you hated it?" I ask, swallowing hard.

"No, not at all. I made a lot of great friends, and it got me here. I have the skills to start my own company. I'm still here with my best friend. It's all good."

That makes me feel a little bit better, and I take another lick of my ice cream.

"What was your favorite thing about the military?"

"The routine. There was no guessing or really that many decisions to be made. There was a chain of command, and everyone knew to follow it. I knew what I was doing every day. I woke up at the same time and ate at the same time. It was the structure that I needed, especially after my childhood."

"Why the Navy?"

"I always liked swimming. There was this community pool by our house, and Anson, Lottie, and I used to break in some nights and go swimming. It was some of our happiest times."

"And then being in the Navy wasn't enough, so you decided to be a SEAL?"

He laughs at that, and I smile.

"Something like that. It was more that I wanted the challenge. Anson and I did it just to see if we could, but having him there is what got me through. I wasn't quitting if he wasn't."

"I'm envious that you have that kind of friend. I always kept to myself, but it would have been nice to have someone who always had my back like that."

"Lottie really likes you," he says, and I smile.

"She was so sweet. She and Anson are adorable together."

"Yeah, they always were. I'm just sorry it took them so long to get together."

Lottie told me all about how she and Anson were scared that Rhett would be mad that they were seeing each other. I remember thinking that was weird. Rhett loves both of them so much, and I know that as long as they're happy, so is he.

"Can I see some of your pictures?" Rhett asks, and I hesitate but nod.

"I only have the ones up on the blog right now," I tell him, and he smiles.

"Let's see."

I pass him my ice cream cone so I can dig my phone out of the clutch. I turn back to see him eyeing my cone, and I laugh.

"You can have some."

"Are you sure?" He asks me, looking like a little boy as he stares down at my ice cream.

"Go for it."

He takes a lick, and my core clenches. It should be an innocent thing. He's just trying my ice cream, but seeing his mouth licking where I was just licking seems so intimate.

"I was worried that it would melt, but it's so cold out here," I joke, and he laughs.

"Are you still cold?" He asks, scooting closer to me in the sand.

"A little, but the coat helps. Thanks for letting me borrow it."

"Of course."

He's such a gentleman, and it seems to come so naturally to him. He saw me shivering and didn't even say anything. Just took off his jacket and draped it over my shoulders without a word.

I pull up the photos and pass him my phone, taking my ice cream cone back.

"Want some of mine?" He offers, and I want to kiss him then, but I nod instead.

"Sure."

He holds the cone out to me, and I lean forward, taking a small lick. The mint and sugar hit my tongue, and I shiver, looking up at him. Our eyes lock, and I can swear that I see hunger in his dark blue eyes.

"It's good," I say and I can feel the blush staining my cheeks.

At least that can warm me up...

Rhett blinks, seeming to come back from his thoughts, and he clears his throat, turning to my phone.

"Whoa," he breathes out as he looks at the first picture. "Where is this?"

"It was this little inlet just up the coast. I stumbled across it when I first got back to town and fell in love with the spot. It's so peaceful there, and there weren't too many people around."

"It looks so zen," he comments, and I smile.

"It was. I'll have to show it to you sometime."

"It's a date," he says easily.

He flips to the next picture, but I'm stuck on his words. Could Rhett really be interested in me? I'm not exactly a model. My mom loves to point out that I could stand to lose some weight. It's always been a source of tension between us, but Rhett doesn't seem to mind the extra weight.

Should I ask him out? For real? Would he think that I was crazy for doing this after we just started our fake relationship? Would he think that I was trying to trick him into dating me?

Rhett is complimenting the next picture, and I paste a smile on my face, trying to ignore the questions swirling in my head.

Just enjoy this time with him. Maybe in a few weeks you can bring it up.

He passes my phone back to me, and our fingers brush. His are freezing cold, and I gasp.

"You're like an ice cube!" I say, pushing to my feet. "Let's go back to my place. It's too cold for this. Can't have you getting sick because of me."

"I'm fine," he says, but he stands too.

"Come on," I say, and this time, I take his hand and lead him over to the car.

We toss the last of our ice cream cones in the trash, and then we're sliding into the car.

"When do you get your car back from the shop?" I ask as he cranks the heat and backs out of the parking lot.

"Tomorrow actually. I have to go there in the morning before I head to the office."

"Big day then," I comment, and he laughs.

"Kind of. We're interviewing some people tomorrow so we can expand Knight Security."

"That's great, Rhett!" I say, twisting in my seat to face him.

"Thanks. We'll have to go out and celebrate if we hire someone," he suggests, and I grin.

"It's a date."

We pull into my apartment's parking lot, and I hesitate when he parks.

"Did you want to come in and warm up a bit?" I ask him, and his eyes darken.

"Uh, sure. That would be great."

He turns off the car, and we head inside in silence. Our eyes lock as the elevator doors start to close, and I lick my lips, wondering if he's as ready to tear my clothes off as I am to do the same to his.

He follows me down the hallway to my apartment, and I shove the key into the lock, turn the knob, and slowly push the door open.

For one breathless moment, it's like we're both weighing our options. I think it's obvious that if he comes in, something will happen between us.

Something real.

Do I want that?

My core clenches, and I know that I have my answer.

I take a step inside, turning to glance at Rhett over my shoulder.

"Maybe I should," he trails off, and I don't know what comes over me.

I can't let him go, though. I want him more than I've ever wanted anything. Before he can say anything else, I reach out, twisting my fingers in his shirt and pulling him towards me. He sways in my direction, and I rise up onto my tiptoes, pressing my lips against his.

"Stay," I murmur against his mouth, and he nods.

Then he's taking over.

His hands clamp down on my hips and he pulls me flush against him. I can feel the hard ridges of his body against mine and my mouth waters. I want to lick him. I want to trace all his scars and muscles with my tongue, memorizing them to my mind.

He backs us up, and I start to trip over my own feet. Before I can fall, Rhett is lifting me up into his arms.

"You'll hurt your back!" I say, and he laughs.

"Wrap your damn legs around me, beautiful," he says, and I giggle as I do what he orders. "Where's the bedroom?"

"Down the hall. The door at the end," I gasp as his hands mold to my ass.

He starts to walk down the hallway, and I squeeze my thighs around him. My fingers tangle in his black hair, and I trail my lips up his neck, biting his earlobe between my teeth lightly.

"Fuck, baby. You're so damn hot," Rhett groans as he finally carries me into the bedroom and over to my bed. "Good thing it's a king size. We're going to need the room."

"Oh, god," I moan.

My core clenches at his words, and I cling to him as he lowers us to the bed. He braces himself on his hands and looks down at me. I stare up at him, trying to read the expression in his dark blue eyes.

"Are you ready for me, baby?" He asks, suddenly so serious, and I nod.

"So ready," I admit, and he smirks.

"Thank fuck."

His lips land back on mine, and I can taste the ice cream when he tangles his tongue with mine. I moan, twinning my arms around his neck as I get lost in him.

I can feel his cock growing between us, and my thighs try to press together but instead just tighten around his waist. It feels like my body is burning up from the inside out, and I start to rock against him, driving both of us crazy.

Rhett's grip on my hair tightens, pulling my head further back, giving himself access to my neck. My back arches, my tits rubbing against his chest through our clothes, and I whine in the back of my throat in need as he licks and nips his way down the column of my neck.

"I want you naked beneath me," Rhett whispers against my skin, and I shiver.

"Yes. I want that too," I practically cry, and he grins down at me.

My breasts feel heavy, and there's an ache between my legs that I can't seem to ease, no matter how tightly I press my thighs together or how much I rub against him. I need more.

His hands are running over me, and I moan and arch into them, nerve endings all over my body coming to life as my clit perks up, eager for attention.

His hands slide around to my back, and I feel him tug down the zipper of my dress. I'm not sure when I ditched his suit jacket, and I can't worry about it now. Not when he's tugging the zipper down, his calloused fingers brushing against my bare skin.

He pulls the dress straps down my arms, and then I'm lying before him in just my bra and panties.

"So, fucking perfect, baby," Rhett says, running one fingertip over the swell of my breast, just above the cup of my bra.

Goosebumps are left in his wake, and I arch up, offering myself to him. I always thought I would be self-conscious being naked in front of someone, but I'm not even focused on that right now. Not with everything that Rhett is doing to me. Not with the way that he's looking at me. The heat in his eyes could burn me alive, and I think that I would love for it to.

Rhett reaches for his shirt, and I almost lose my patience watching him undo all those dang buttons.

We lose the rest of our clothes in a blur of fumbles and rushed movements. His cock rubs along my skin, hot and heavy between my legs, and my hips lift, needing him to move just a little bit lower.

Almost there...

My head is thrown back on the pillow, and my hands fist in the sheets as I try to rock against him, but he keeps evading me. He trails kisses down my neck and chest, and I gasp when his lips wrap around the stiff peak of one of my nipples. I cry out, arching into him further in an attempt to get him to take more into his mouth.

"So greedy," he says, sounding pleased, and I close my eyes, getting lost in the sensations.

His tongue teases the sensitive bud, and heat pools between my thighs. When the head of his cock dips lower, bumping over my clit, I'm sure I'm about to come. He's not even inside me yet, and I'm already so close to the edge.

"Fuck, I love your body," he groans against the swell of one breast.

I can only moan as he kisses his way to the other one, taking that nipple into his mouth to tease it with his tongue. He licks and sucks until they're red and puffy, so sensitive that I think I would combust if the wind blew across them. They're wet from his mouth, and when I look down, I can see that my chest is flushed a rosy pink.

"Spread those pretty thighs. I need to taste you right now. I want your flavor in my mouth when I fuck you the first time."

I spread my legs enthusiastically as Rhett kisses over the soft swell of my stomach and settles between my thighs.

"So pretty and pink," he says as his thumbs spread my lower lips, exposing all of me to him.

I'm about to beg him to taste me when he leans in and takes one long slow lick up my center. My head thrashes on the pillow as Rhett's tongue licks up and down my slit, spreading me with the tip of his tongue and circling my sensitive button.

My hips move against his mouth as my orgasm grows bigger and bigger inside of me.

"Give it to me, Quinn. Drench my face with these sweet juices. I want you to come all over me," Rhett growls against my soaked core, and I almost sob as the first wave of my orgasm hits me.

"Rhett!" I scream as I come against list his mouth.

His tongue licks up all of my cream, his thumb working my clit as he tries to prolong my release.

When my body goes slack, he gives me one last lick

before he looks up, his eyes meeting mine. I can't wait any longer.

I grab his arm, dragging him up my body and then pulling him down until his mouth meets mine. I kiss him hard, tasting my release on his lips as I shift beneath him, urging him to slip inside me.

Rhett's hands run down my body, his palms cupping my plump ass as he yanks me forward, thrusting into me in one swift move. He seats himself fully inside me, and I gasp, wincing as I struggle to get used to his cock stretching me so wide around him.

I probably should have told him I was a virgin, but it's too late for that now.

"Fuck, Quinn," Rhett grits out, a pained expression etched onto his handsome face.

"Just give me a second. I'll be alright," I tell him, and already I can feel the pain starting to fade as pleasure takes its place.

When I start to shift under him, he takes that as his cue and begins to move. He's slow at first, letting me get used to the new sensations. When I wrap my legs around his waist, digging my heels into his ass and urging him to go faster, harder.

I gasp when he gives me what I want, pounding into me as his fingers dig into my ass. My arms wrap around his neck, and I hold onto him as that familiar pulsing feeling starts to grow inside of me.

"Rhett, Rhett, Rhett," I chant as he angles my hips up so that he can brush against my clit with each pass.

Tingles start to grow stronger, and my hands slip to his shoulders, my short nails digging into his muscles as I start to splinter apart around him.

"Yes! Rhett!" I scream as I come, my back arching and

my legs tightening around his hips as I come all over his cock.

Rhett's hips piston into me as he swells and starts to come inside me. His body shakes as his release splashes inside of me.

"Quinn," he groans against my neck as his release subsides.

We're both breathing hard as Rhett pulls out of me slowly and then collapses next to me on the bed. When I finally come back down, I realize I'm smiling like a love-drunk fool and try to school my features.

I can't let him know that I'm falling in love with him.

Some of the magic starts to fade as I realize I just slept with my fake boyfriend but then Rhett is there, looming over me.

"All good?" He asks me, and I smile.

"Ready for more."

He grins down at me before his body covers mine once more.

NINE

Rhett

I WAKE up with Quinn sprawled naked across my chest, her pale blonde hair tickling my chin, and it's the most amazing way to wake up in the world. I grin to myself, kissing the top of her head and breathing in her sweet honeysuckle scent.

Now I know that she tastes as good as she smells, I think with a smirk as I wrap my arms tighter around her.

My phone starts to ring on the bedside table, and I ignore it. I don't want anything to pull me from this bubble with my girl, but when I look towards the window, I notice that the sun is pretty high up.

"Shit," I whisper, silently groaning as I realize I must be late for today's interviews.

I hate to just slip out, but she looks so peaceful sleeping, and I don't want to wake her. I know I kept her up late last night, and she could probably use the rest so as gently as possible, I slip out from under her and tuck the covers around her so she doesn't get cold.

She reaches her hand out like she's looking for me, and I want nothing more than to crawl back into bed and wake her up with my tongue between her legs, but I'm already running late so I settle for kissing her forehead before going in search of my clothes.

I get dressed as quickly as possible and head out the door. I forgot that I have to stop at the mechanic and pick up my truck, and I curse as I ride the elevator down to the ground floor and jog over to my car.

I send a quick text to Anson that I'm on my way and will be there soon and then send another text to Quinn.

RHETT: **Last night was amazing, beautiful. I had to go get my car and head into work. Call me when you wake up.**

AS SOON AS I hit send, I wonder if that was too much. I'm treating this like we're a real couple, like last night meant something to both of us, but what if that's not true? What if last night was just her blowing off steam? What if she just got caught up in the moment?

I'm going to drive myself crazy thinking about it. I need to talk to Quinn and lay all my cards on the table. I need to find out where we stand.

I'll do it as soon as the interviews are over, I promise myself.

I battle the traffic to the mechanic shop and exchange

keys with them before I drive my now-fixed car over to the Knight Security offices.

"Sorry that I'm late," I say as I rush inside.

Anson is in his office, and I see the back of two men in there with me.

"Have we already started the interview?" I ask, grinding to a halt as I realize that I recognize the two interviewees.

"Kye? Gates?" I ask, grinning as I move to clap my friends on the back.

Kye laughs as he hugs me back, and I grin as I do the same to Gates.

"You two got out too?" I ask them as we all drop into chairs in Anson's office.

"Yeah, just a few weeks ago, actually," Kye says.

Anson and I were in the SEALs with Kye and Gates. We've been on more than a few deployments with them. I hadn't heard from them since just after I was sent home. They were still overseas on their own deployment.

"Didn't want to go on another deployment?" I guess, and they nod.

"It got worse after you were sent back," Kye admits, and we have a moment of silence as that sinks in for all of us.

They don't need to elaborate or give any more details. Anson and I both noticed the increased danger with every deployment. We knew it was only a matter of time before one of us was hurt or worse.

"Are you settling in Los Angeles?" I ask, and they nod.

"We went up and visited Hunter and Whit for a week and thought about moving there, but it's such a small town. I need a little more excitement than that," Kye says, and I laugh.

"I bet. We just helped Hunter and Whit out with something a few weeks ago actually. They sound like they're fully at home up there, though."

Hunter and Whit were in the military with us too. They got out a few months ago and promptly moved into their own cabins on the side of a mountain. They live in this little town up there which would drive me bonkers, but they seem to love it. They met their girls, Anise and Grier, there and are now happily in love.

"Yeah, they're both married now, which is crazy to me," Kye says, and Gates grunts in agreement.

That's how things always are with these two. Kye is the charmer, the guy who can be friends with anyone. Gates is more the grumpy silent type–the one where you never quite know what he's thinking.

"Where are you guys staying?" Anson asks.

"We rented this condo a few blocks from here," Kye says, nodding north.

"Oh, cool. My place is over there, too," I comment.

"Yeah, what's been new with you two?" Kye asks.

"I'm with Lottie now, and she's pregnant," Anson says with a smile, and Kye grins.

"About damn time," Gates grumbles, and I laugh.

"That's what I said too. All that wasted time," I chide Anson, and he rolls his eyes.

"It was the right time now."

I nod, and Kye turns to me.

"I've been seeing this girl, Quinn."

"Is it serious?" He asks, and I nod.

"Yeah, she's it for me."

Anson claps me on the shoulder, grinning, and I laugh.

"Maybe there will be two weddings soon," Anson says, and I smile.

"Maybe."

If I can get Quinn to realize that we're meant to be and then somehow convince her to spend the rest of her life with me.

"I'll get my best man speeches ready then," Kye teases, and I laugh, leaning back in my chair.

"Should we get on with the interview?" Anson asks, and I grin.

I know he's about to give them shit, but of course, we'll hire them. Kye and Gates are two guys we trust and love having around.

Kye was a great breacher, and he's always been good with computers so I know he'll be a great addition to the team. Gates was a medic, but he's extremely proficient with any firearm. He'll be good in a bad situation, and he's like a brick wall so maybe just the sight of the grumpy giant will be enough to deter any threats.

"If hired," Anson starts, and I laugh. "What would you bring to the team?"

"Guns," Gates says with a straight face, and I laugh silently.

"What would you say is your biggest weakness?" Anson asks, and I cover my face with my hand.

"My intolerance for assholes," Gate deadpans, staring straight at Anson, and I lose it.

Anson grins, and I know that the interview is over. I'm surprised that he asked more than one question, if I'm being honest.

"When do we start?" Gates asks.

"Tomorrow. We have a new client that we'll be working on starting tomorrow morning so be here bright and early."

"You got it, boss," Kye says, and I lean back in my chair. "Is it lunchtime yet?"

"Yes," I say, pushing to my feet.

"Where are we going?"

"Burgers," Gates says, and I look at Anson, shrugging.

"Works for me."

Gates phone dings and he pulls it out.

"Who the heck is texting you? Everyone that you like is in this room," Kye jokes and Gates rolls his eyes.

"It's Dillon," he says in that gruff voice of his.

"Ah, the girlfriend," Kye says and I grin.

"Not my girlfriend. Girl. Friend," Gate stresses.

Dillon and Gates have been friends for forever. It was a well known fact that he was in love with her, but he has yet to make a move on her.

"She might be coming to Los Angeles," Gates says as he texts her back.

"Is that why we moved here?" Kye asks, looking outraged. "I'm battling hours of traffic everyday so that you *might* be in the same city as your girl friend who is not your *girlfriend?*"

Gates just shrugs, already heading for the door. Kye is still giving him shit as Anson locks the door and I can't help but laugh.

Man, I didn't realize how much I missed them.

I smile as I head out with my friends, but the whole time, I'm rehearsing what I want to say to Quinn when I see her.

"Hey, it will be okay," Anson tells me quietly as we head over to our cars.

"What?" I ask, blinking up at him.

"Whatever you're freaking out about. It will be okay."

He claps me on the back, and I smile as I climb into my car.

He's right. It will all work out.

Because I won't accept any other outcome.

TEN

Quinn

WHEN I WAKE UP ALONE, I almost think I dreamt last night, but I know from my sore muscles that it happened. The other side of the bed is cold, and I know that Rhett has been up and gone for some time.

"Ugh," I groan as I stretch, trying to ease some of the aches in my muscles.

I need to start working out if I want to be able to handle him more than once a week, I think to myself with a giggle.

I pull myself out of the bed and pad into the bathroom, turning on the shower and cranking it as hot as it will go. It isn't until I'm standing under the spray, the sleep cleared from my brain, that I realize I might be reading too much into last night.

I stand under the hot water, replaying last night over and over in my head. It had been good. Really good. I know that I don't have anything to compare it to, but the fact that I almost blacked out has to mean something, right?

Good sex doesn't mean that we're in love or that he wants to make this relationship real, though.

I need to talk to him.

I could go to Knight Security, except isn't he interviewing today? And his car was done and ready for pick up. I don't even know if he'll still be at work, and I never got his address so I can't go knock on his door.

This feels like a conversation that needs to be had in person, and not over the phone, so I guess I'll have to wait.

I climb out of the shower and dry off. I already know that I'll be staying in today. I need to edit some of the pictures I took the other day, and maybe that will help keep my mind off of Rhett and this whole crazy fake relationship.

I grab my phone on my way into the closet and smile when I see that Rhett texted me. He must have sent it right after he left because it's from a few hours ago. I'm surprised to see that it's already close to two in the afternoon.

I guess I really needed the sleep.

I've never slept in this late in my life, and I get a secret thrill that I've done it now. My parents would for sure call Rhett a bad influence, a proper lady never sleeps in past noon, after all, but I kind of love that he's corrupting me.

I've been getting to experience so many new things since I met Rhett. He's brought me out of the boring, bland bubble that my parents put me in and that I've been too scared to leave. He's shown me that there's so much more to life than money and stuffy parties.

What's more, I like who I am with him. He makes me laugh and smile like no one ever has. He makes me feel precious and cherished. I always thought of myself as average looking, but through Rhett's eyes, I'm the most beautiful woman in the world.

He wouldn't do all of that if he didn't like me too. Would he?

It's hard to tell because he's such a good guy. I'm sure that he makes everyone he meets feel at ease and seen.

"Ugh, I'm going to drive myself crazy analyzing all of this," I groan out loud. "Put it out of your head. Let's just get dressed and get some work done."

My stomach is too in knots to try to eat anything right now so I pull on my comfiest sweater and yoga pants and head over to the couch. I grab my computer and settle in. All the pictures are already loaded from my camera, and I flip through them, deciding which ones to edit for the blog and social media.

I try to get lost in work, but every picture makes me think of Rhett.

I should show him this place.

I wonder if Rhett would think that statue was cool.

I bet Rhett would have made this shot better. I could have asked him to take his shirt off and stand in the surf.

Great, now I'm turned on.

It goes on like that for another hour before I give up and start to pace around my apartment. It's close to five now, and he should be getting off work any minute.

Should I text him? Or maybe I could call him and see if he can come over or if we can meet somewhere?

Scratch that. We should definitely do this in private. If things don't go well, I don't want to cry in front of many people.

I head back to the couch to grab my phone when it starts to ring. My heart leaps for one second and I hope it's Rhett.

Mom flashes at me on the screen, and I hit ignore. A knock sounds at the door, and I look down at my outfit.

Would my parents come out here? Probably. I've been avoiding their calls for the past few days.

I straighten my shoulders and paste a smile on my face as I head to answer the door.

"Oh, thank god," I gasp when I see Rhett standing there instead of my mom and dad.

"Uh, is everything okay?" He asks.

"Yeah, I thought that it was my parents knocking. I really didn't want to deal with them today."

"Understandable," he says, and I grin.

"Come in. I was actually hoping that you would stop by. I needed to talk to you."

"What a coincidence, because I need to talk to you too," he says, and the relief I felt at seeing him quickly evaporates.

"You go first," I say, chickening out.

"Okay."

He takes a deep breath, looking like he's giving himself an internal pep talk, and I wonder what he could be so nervous about.

Oh, no. He's met someone and wants to call this fake relationship off. Or he doesn't think we should sleep together again and is trying to let me down easily. Or—

"I want you to be more than my fake girlfriend," he says, interrupting my internal freak-out.

"What's that?" I ask.

There's no way that I could have heard him right. Maybe I'm dreaming right now.

"I know that when we started this, we said it would be fake, but I don't want that anymore. Hell, I never wanted that. I wanted to ask you out that first day when you hit me with your car, but you seemed so stressed out, and I didn't want to add to that. Then you called and sprung this crazy idea on me."

"It's not that crazy," I mumble, shifting on my feet, and he laughs.

"It was bonkers, Quinn."

"You said yes to it!"

"Yeah, because I wanted you any way I could get you," he says with a wide smile.

My phone starts to ring again. Mom. Again.

I hit ignore and look back to Rhett.

"So, you want to be with a crazy person," I say, and he laughs.

"More than anything, but what do you want?"

My phone starts to ring again, and I groan.

"I'm sorry," I start, but he holds up his hand.

"It's okay. Answer it before they show up here."

We both shiver at that thought, and I take a deep breath before I raise the phone to my ear.

"Hello?"

"There you are! We've been trying to call you, young lady," my mom snaps.

"What's up?"

"We've set up a dinner party tonight with Tripp and his parents. We expect you to be here within the hour," she says primly, and something in me snaps.

I'm never going to be happy being who my parents want me to be. I want to live my own life, and it's obvious that they're not on board with that.

I look to Rhett for strength in telling my mom no for the first time in my life, and I can see the anxiety coming off of him. He's nervous, and I realize I never told him how I felt about him. He just poured his heart out to me, and I left him hanging.

I take another deep breath, and my eyes lock with his dark blue ones.

"Actually, mom. I can't make dinner tonight with them. Or any night."

She starts to sputter, and I smile softly.

"I'm in love with Rhett, so I don't want to be set up with any more of your friends' sons. I choose him," I say, and he's on me in an instant.

I laugh, hanging up on whatever my mom is saying as he tilts my head up. His lips claim mine in the next instant, and I sink into his embrace, only for him to pull away in the next breath.

"I love you too, Quinn."

"Crazy in love," I say, and he laughs, wrapping his arms around me as his lips find mine once more.

ELEVEN

Rhett

I GATHER Quinn up in my arms and carry her back to her bedroom. I want to lay her out and have her tell me that she loves me over and over again, but it appears that Quinn has other ideas.

"I wanted to try something," she admits, a wicked light in her green eyes.

"What?" I ask, and I honestly don't have a clue what she means until she drops to her knees in front of me. "Fuck!"

She looks up at me, her eyes wide and filled with surprise as she stares up at me.

"You don't like this?" She asks, and I swallow hard.

"Baby, I'll love anything that you do to me. You don't have to do this though."

"I want to," she insists, and I'm powerless to tell her no.

Her hands go to the button and zipper of my suit pants, and she tugs them down. I should have gone home and changed after work, but I was too anxious to talk to Quinn and get everything out in the open. I was driving myself crazy, wondering how she was going to react to my wanting more.

Her hand reaches into my boxers, and I groan as her fingers wrap around my length. The head bobs in front of her face, and when I see her lick her lips, I grit my teeth to stop from coming all over her face.

"Easy," I caution her as she shifts on her knees, and she smirks up at me.

Then she's opening around me. She swallows half my length on the first try, and my hips buck, forcing another inch into her mouth.

"Shit, sorry," I gasp, but she just swallows around me, blinking those green eyes up at me innocently.

She swallows again, and my eyes almost roll back in my head.

"Do you not have a gag reflex, baby?" I pant, and she shrugs, my cock stretching her lips. "Fuck, I'm one lucky bastard."

She glides her lips up and down my cock, her hand joining and wrapping around my length to work in time with her mouth. Her fucking magical mouth.

My balls start to draw up, and tingles race up my spine. I know then that I need to get her to stop if I want to fuck her.

"My turn, baby," I growl, and she smirks as I reach down and pull her to her feet.

I grab her, throwing her down on the bed, my hands already reaching for her yoga pants, and I drag them and her panties down her legs. She spreads her legs without me having to say a word, and I reward her by burying my face in her sweet folds.

"Rhett!" She screams, and I swirl my tongue around her clit harder.

She's already soaked for me, and I wonder if sucking my cock turned her on. I push one finger into her snug channel, and she arches off the bed, trying to take me deeper. I love how greedy she always is for me, and I add a second finger, stretching her wider as I tease her clit.

"Please," she begs, and I take one last lick before I climb up her body and thrust into her.

She screams my name, and I can feel my orgasm already starting to brew inside me. She's so tight, so hot and wet, like silk wrapped around me. It's the best thing that I've ever felt in my life.

I wanted to make love to her, to take things nice and slow, but as soon as I'm balls deep inside her, that plan goes out the window.

It's like she's trying to suck the come from me, and I grit my teeth so I don't come too fast.

"It's so good," Quinn moans, and I close my eyes.

"Say it again," I order as I lean back, angling my hips to hit her g-spot with each thrust.

"So good," she says, and then I see her blink. "I love you," she says, giving me what I want.

"I love you too," I tell her.

I bow my head, my lips claiming hers as we both start to come. I swallow her release, my name tasting like heaven on her lips.

"Fuck," I hiss as her walls clamp tight around me.

Quinn lets out a breathy sigh and smiles almost drunkenly up at me.

"I love you, beautiful," I whisper, leaning on my elbows to kiss her.

"I know. I love you too."

"I think I'm going to keep saying it until it feels real," I admit, and she laughs.

"It always felt real," she whispers, and I smile.

"Yeah, it did."

She kisses me again, and my cock hardens inside her, ready for round two already.

TWELVE

Quinn

FIVE YEARS LATER...

"ARE you ready for our next adventure?" Rhett asks as he wheels me into the hospital.

"So ready," I say with a grin.

That smile quickly crumbles when another contraction hits me.

"Breathe, baby," Rhett encourages me, letting me squeeze his hand as the pain increases.

"Checking in?" The nurse at the front counter jokes, smiling sweetly, and I nod.

She passes Rhett some papers to fill out as another nurse comes over to wheel me down to a room. Rhett is right by my side, constantly saying encouraging words as I'm moved over to the hospital bed.

Rhett and I have spent the last five years traveling the world together. We've been all over, and it's been amazing. My travel blog has taken off, and I know that I owe a large chunk of my success to Rhett. He gave me the courage to travel and chase my dreams. He's been nothing but supportive of my blog and everything else that I wanted to do in life.

We got married a month after we made things official. By then, we were both head over heels for each other, and I knew he was the one for me. He proposed at our spot on the beach, and I had almost tackled him into the sand when I said yes.

We just had a courthouse wedding, something that upset my parents to no end. They weren't happy with my choice of husband, and we haven't talked much since we got married. They've started to come around recently, though, and I'm sure it has more to do with their future grandchild than a true change of heart. Either way, Rhett and I have agreed to keep them at arm's length for now.

Rhett and Anson's security company has really taken off in the last five years, and they've expanded their operation quite a bit. They hired Gates and Kye, two of their military friends, before we left on our honeymoon. Since then, those two, and their now wives, have become like family to me.

Speaking of family...

"How is she doing?" Lottie asks as she and Anson rush in, their little one in their arms.

"I'm fine," I promise them.

"How is she?" Kye asks, appearing at the door with the biggest teddy bear I've ever seen.

Gates is right behind him with a huge bouquet of flowers.

"Do you need anything?" He asks us, and I shake my head as another contraction hits.

"Dillon and Aria said they're on their way," Kye says, reading the text off his phone. "They want to know if you need anything too."

"We're fine."

The doctor bustles in, takes one look at the crowded room, and laughs.

"I'm afraid that everyone who isn't a birthing partner will have to wait in the lobby now," she says, and all of our friends wave, offering words of encouragement and promising to be just outside as they leave.

"Are you ready to meet your little one?" Dr. Miller asks, and I smile.

"So ready."

When Rhett and I found out we were expecting, it was a bit of a shock. I had only just gone off birth control and thought it would take longer than a month to get pregnant.

We had decided that now was the time to start trying for a family. Seeing Anson and Lottie with their kids had me yearning for kids of my own. The blog was doing well, and we can still travel, or I can pivot and start doing photo shoots around here. For the time being, I'm really just looking forward to bonding with our baby.

"Let's check things out," Dr. Miller says, and Rhett takes my hand as she lifts the sheet.

"I love you," I tell him, and he grins.

"Good, 'cause I love you too."

I don't know why I thought that car accident was such a bad thing that day. It turned out to be the best thing that ever happened to me.

I'm just glad that Rhett is a little bit crazy, just like me, and agreed to my fake dating plan.

I know that with him by my side, we'll be able to tackle any adventure.

***

Curious about Anson and Lottie's story? Check out A Baby For The Navy SEAL!

ABOUT THE AUTHOR

CONNECT WITH ME!

If you enjoyed this story, please consider leaving a review on Amazon or any other reader site or blog that you like. Don't forget to recommend it to your other reader friends.

If you want to chat with me, please consider joining my VIP list or connecting with me on one of my Social Media platforms. I love talking with each of my readers. Links below!

<u>Website</u>
<u>Newsletter</u>

A Very Mountain Man Christmas

A Very Mountain Man New Year

Folklore

Kidnapping His Forever

Claiming His Forever

Finding His Forever

Rescuing His Forever

Chasing His Forever

Folklore: The Complete Series

Holiday Hearts

Be Mine

Falling in Love

Holly Jolly Holidays

Love Notes

Signing Off With Love

Care Package Love

Wrong Number, Right Love

Kings Gym

Fighting Fire With Fire

Fighting Tooth and Nail

Fighting Back From Hell

Mine To

Mine to Love

Mine to Protect

Mine to Cherish

Mine to Keep

Mine to: The Complete Series

Sequoia: Stud Farm

Branded

Bucked

Roped

Spurred

Sequoia: Fast Love Racing

Jump Start

Pit Stop

Home Stretch

Telltale Heart

Bought and Paid For

His Miracle

Pretty Girl

Telltale Hearts Boxset